*To John and Ann Brantingham for their nonpareil friendship, their enthusiasm for my novellas, their professionalism in the hosting of readings for me, and for exemplifying the humanitarian qualities to which we all might well aspire.*

*And to D.H. Lloyd, of Applezaba Press, who also embodied the qualities to which I allude above, and to whom I owe a debt of gratitude for having published the original edition of this work in 1984.*

*And to Shane Rhodes of Wrecking Ball Press, who with the assistance of my dear friend and supporter Dr. Jules Smith, published the English edition of the work in 1999.*

# Acknowledgements

*The Case Of The Missing Blue Volkswagen* was previously published in 1984 by Applezaba Press (USA) and in 1999 by Wrecking Ball Press (UK). A German translation of this work appeared from Maro Verlag and from Bertelsmann Verlag in 1985-86.

# Foreward

When I was twenty five, I wanted something different.

I'd read books voraciously all my life. I grew up with bouts of near deafness that left me without the company of anything but books. So, by that time, I'd read the classics and the modernists. I'd read a lot of newer authors and a good deal of the post modernists. I spent some time with Kurt Vonnegut and Jack Kerouac as all young men do and should, and I'd been enamored of Hemingway, Bukowski, Pynchon, Steinbeck, and Delillo.

I loved all of these people, but I wanted something new.

It was then that I stumbled onto Gerry Locklin's work, and *The Case of the Missing Blue Volkswagen* was the first of his I read. I had just been accepted into the MFA at Cal State Long Beach, and I wanted a sense of who was teaching there. All of what I read, I enjoyed, and I could see I had a lot to gain from the experience, but something about what Locklin was doing with prose knocked me over.

He was playing with genre with a style that was post-modern, but with a difference. I'd always liked detective fiction, and if his novella had been a mere parody, it would have turned me off. It was more than that.

What I realized was that Locklin is using style and structure to have a conversation with his readers about what the limits of fiction are. And he's telling us is the limits we've placed on our work are too restrictive.

And so the great teacher of so many students in LA was teaching us once again.

What did he teach us?

That chapters do not need to be long to have meaning.

That a single moment written well suggests a lifetime. It can suggest a philosophy too.

That absurdity can reveal truth.

That genre novels are filled with beauty and truth.

That the delving into the subconscious and pain does not need to be maudlin.

That maguffins, framing devices, settings, and plots can be all secondary to characters.

That if Hemingway, Kerouac, and Steinbeck were the voices that revealed the truths, terrors, and inanities of their generations and places, Locklin is one of the most central and important voices of his, and that if we want to understand the mindset and chaos of the late 20th century, we need only to look at what he has done. No one can understand the artistic movements of Los Angeles without first understand his work.

I wanted to find something different when I was twenty-five. I wanted someone to speak to my experience, and although I have never wandered the streets of Long Beach or Los Angeles searching for a mythical blue Volkswagen, his book spoke to me in a way that no other book ever had.

I know you will enjoy this.

--John Brantingham, author of
*Let Us All Pray Now to Our
Own Strange Gods*

# The Broad

She came into my office like a broad in one of those hard-boiled detective flicks. Lauren Bacall, maybe. Or Charlotte Rampling. All of them.

I had no idea what color her hair was, let alone her eyes. I'm just not very observant. Even when I have nothing better to do than observe.

That's one of the myths of private detectives, that we're all highly observant. I'm the best and about half the time I don't recognize my own hand when I'm blowing my nose. I know one dick who carries his license plate number written down in his wallet so he can find his car in the lot after work.

There's not much point in wasting a lot of time noticing details. Murderers—they're all alike. Women—they're all alike. Victims—they're all alike. Women-murderers, women-victims…

Yawn.

## The Office

It's a mess. It's not a myth that private detectives' offices are always a mess. They are universally a mess, even in Communist China where messiness is akin to treason.

In my own case, I used to be a reasonably neat person and an utter failure as a dick until one day I read in the paper that someone had done a study and it turned out the only factor he could isolate as a possible common denominator of geniuses was the capacity for tolerating clutter.

That day I began to let the shit collect around here.

I could feel my IQ rising at the rate of one point for every inch of debris.

Now I am neither neat nor observant but I'm bright.

## If You're So Goddam Smart Then Why Aren't You Rich?

Isn't that the most infuriating question?

I suppose I never set out to get rich in the first place, and I suppose I devote too much attention to doing my job well and not enough to investing my earnings, and this isn't as highly paid a profession as you might imagine anyway, and who knows, maybe I **will** be rich someday.

## Well You Could At Least Give Us Some Idea What The Broad Looked Like

She was long, lean, and sexy; her clothes fit tight; a certain amount of bosom and thigh was showing.

I like 'em that way.

It's not the only way I like 'em, but I do like 'em that way.

## What Were You Doing When The Broad Came Into Your Office

I was reading a book called **The Dick** by Bruce Jay Friedman. It's a great book, funny and dirty and one of the few in contemporary literature in which the hero gets his shit together and makes a life for himself and those dear to him.

The only trouble is whenever I hear the term **dick** now, I think of Friedman's book. And the term pops up quite a bit in my line of work.

If you've read that book, you may already be having trouble with this one.

Well, what the fuck do you expect me to do about it?

# What Did The Broad Want?

After I got her settled into a chair at the most advantageous angle for my looking up her skirt, I asked her that very question.

She said, "I want you to find my missing blue Volkswagen."

"What is it missing?" I asked.

"It's not missing anything, you idiot. I'm missing **it**!

"How strange," I continued, since I find it difficult not to fall into an occasional Grouch, "I've heard of women missing their dogs or their lovers, very seldom their husbands, though, and never their Volkswagens. A Porsche I could understand."

"MY VOLKSWAGEN HAS BEEN STOLEN, YOU NINCOMPOOP! I WANT YOU TO GET MY MISSING BLUE VOLKSWAGEN BACK FOR ME!"

"Okay, okay, you don't have to shout at me. All my life people have been shouting at me. What for? I'm a good boy, I've even gotten pretty bright, and …"

"Look, can you get my car back for me?"

"Of course."

"Fine. When can you get started on the case?"

"What's wrong with right now?"

"Don't you have any other cases?"

"I don't remember. Incidentally, if I'm such an idiot, why did you come to me instead of some other dick?"

"**Dick**," she said, "you know whenever I hear that word I think of Friedman's book. But, anyway, I came to you because I heard you were the best."

# Getting Down To Brass Tacks

"Okay," I said, how long has the car been missing?"

"I don't really know. I went to bed for a few days, got into a fetal position, sweated a lot, went kind of crazy, and when I finally emerged from my withdrawal, the car was gone."

"Where was it parked?"

"I don't remember that either. You see, I had been hitting the bars steadily for a week trying to lose my virginity."

**"You're a virgin?"**

"That's right. And I decided it was damn well time I got over being one. So I went out to the bars, and I made myself available to the guys, and a lot of them I even sidled up to, and a number of them talked dirty to me and some of them even felt me up, but sooner or later they'd catch on that I **wanted** them, and **why** I wanted them, and they, they just sort of lost interest."

"Well at least we won't have to go looking for your maidenhead too, ha ha, but, by the way, where do you live?"

"I forgot that on the way over here."

"That's perfectly natural," I said. "Why don't you just go looking for the place you live in, while I see what I can do about tracking down your car. What color did you say it was?"

"It's a blue VW."

"What year?"

"It's old."

"Excellent. With that and all the other information you've given me, I shouldn't have any trouble finding it at all."

## A Logical Starting Point

I decided the most likely place to start looking would be in a bar. So I drove down to Seal Beach where Paul was working.

I explained my plight to him and he said, "Have you ever noticed that Orientals always drive yellow cars?"

"I hadn't noticed that."

"You keep your eyes open from now on and you'll see I'm right."

He washed a few beer glasses and came back to me: "And I've never met a man who owned a Porsche who wasn't a total asshole."

# The Wisdom of Paul/The Wisdom of the East
## Or Paint Your Wagen

I sat there drinking Seagram's Seven and Coke, which goes down great but really fucks me up, my stomach especially, in the long run, and suddenly it came to me that Paul was right.

So I finished my drink and drove straight to Chinatown.

I searched the area for a Volkswagen recently painted yellow.

Nary a one to be found.

Finally I was approached by a fat, gangster-type slant-eye. "No tickee, no washee," he said.

"Jesus," I replied, "what did you say that for? That doesn't make any sense at all."

"Oh," he said, "sorry. I thought you were scouting locations for a remake of Chinatown. I missed them the first time around. I was back in Tokyo tending to my Farmer Sukiyaki Hot Dog franchise."

I raised my eyebrows. I tried to raise just the left one, but, as usual, they both came up. "Tokyo?" I pregnantly inquired.

"Oh shit yes, we all the same. Nip, chink, Seoul-brothers, all us yellow bastards. We velly similar, not even able to tell each other apart. We all great movie actors though. You make karate film, perhaps? Samurai? Anti-Vietnam? Dragon-lady? Documentary of Chairman Mao? Chiang-Kai-Shecky?..."

"Nah," I said, "I'm just looking for a stolen car."

"Velly solly, but no clime in Chinatown."

"Bullshit," I said, "Chinatown is one of the great clime—I mean crime—centers of the world. Everyone knows that."

"Okay," he said, "you win, you Yankee toughguys too smart and unrelenting for poor former coolie presently engaged in fast-food franchising. I tell you truth: streets overrun with stolen Datsuns, Toyotas, Mazdas, Hondas, and rickshaws, but no Volkswagens. German workmanship big fat knockwurst of a myth."

I looked about me and sure enough, the curbs were lined with Datsuns, Toyotas, Mazdas, Hondas, and a surprisingly large number of rickshaws—all of them yellow.

## Chop Suey

"Hey, pal," he whispered in my face, his breath reeking of garlic, "you wanna foke my seester?"

"Christ, man, that's the Mexicans. The Orientals have a cohesive family structure."

"More folklore," he said, "c'mon-a my house a-my-yai house, I'm a gonna a-give-a you Ca-an-dy..."

"That was written by William Saroyan," I said. "He's an Armenian.

"Yeah, but my sister's name really is Candy and she really is a virgin."

"No shit."

"I shit you not."

"Well, I don't know. In the books, Philip Marlowe never went to bed with women. It's only in the screen adaptations that he always gets laid."

"Philip Marlowe get nooky one time."

"Come to think of it, that's right...it happened in..."

"What we stand around like a couple of UCLA reference librarians for? You come up and nibble a little authentic Schzechwan-Mandarin-Cantonese chop suey."

"Well, maybe just this once..."

"Better have seconds. Not stick to ribs."

# Candy My Ass

Candy My Ass, is right.  In the upstairs room
I was set upon by four thugs just graduated from
Sumo U.  They strapped me to a chair and said,
"Talk!"

"Okay," I said, "Testing—One, Two, Three,
Four…"

That got me a couple of hammy fists in the
gut.

"All right, smart boy," said the skinniest one
of the bunch, and he vaguely resembled Ming the
Malevolent.  "You'll talk when we get through
giving you the needle."

So they gave me the needle.  Literally.  They
gave me a dose a million Chinese poppy farmers
must have labored to produce.  Then they waited for
a reaction.  There was none.

"Let him have another of the same," the
svelte one ordered.

His cohorts eyed him in dismay.  "Jesus,
Telly, another one of those will croak him for sure."

"GIVE IT TO HIM!"

"Okay, okay, you don't have to yell."

They shot me again and waited.

Nothing happened.

"Hey, buddy," said the one recently addressed
as Telly, "you already have a hype or something?"

"I never touch the stuff."

"Do you take a lot of pills? A lot of downers maybe?"

"Oh, once in a while I'll take some sleeping pills for insomnia. If you don't sleep tonight, tomorrow you won't function right."

"How many of those sleeping pills might you take at one time?"

"Oh, five or six hundred."

"Six hundred sleeping pills? How long do you sleep?

"To tell you the truth, I missed the greater part of 1969."

## In Memory of Malcolm Lowry

They gave up on the dope trick. Instead, they took a quart of Seagram's Seven Crown and forced it down my throat.

"Wait a second, wait a second," I managed to gurgle, "you don't have to do that. How perceptive of you to have chosen my brand. None of the bite of the bourbons, and the Canadians give me a headache. Scotch is one of the most expensive hoaxes ever foisted on the **nouveau-riche**. If you'd be so kind as to provide me with a little Seven-Up or Canada Dry Ginger Ale, I'd be pleased to drink to your heart's content."

"Hey, Kremlin," barked Telly, "run down to Deli Sukiyaki and bring back a case of their cheapest lemon-lime."

Kremlin, whose shoulders were just a little wider than the Verrazano-Narrows bridge, disappeared down the stairs.

I knew the ersatz Seven was going to taste like shit, but what the hell, I was a guest in the dungeon of friends.

Eventually, I drank about eleven hundred Seven-Sevens. After the umpteenth case of lemon-lime, Kremlin looked at Telly and said, "Boss, we over our credit limit on both Visa and Master Charge."

Telly looked at me and said, "Okay, smart boy, you pretty smart boy for a person with such scrunched-up eyes. I let you go this time. You promise never to come back?"

"I don't like chow mein anyway."

"Who does? I only eat prime rib. Recommend Lawry's. Be sure wear sport coat—no get in without one. Incidentally, in going through pockets of you present garb, it come to our attention you no carry gun."

"I never learned to shoot one. Anyway, I never have any occasion to use one. That's one of the myths of our profession—that you're always getting into situations where a gun would come in handy."

"Well, I sure hate to see Best Dick running around without a gun. Just don't look right. You owe something, you know, to your fans, to us of the underworld, to little children all over America. Take my own kids, for instance, they shit their little pants if they find out that Best Dick no carry gun. Here, we take up little collection for going-away present. Almost-bland-new .38, one owner, now deceased. You take this and nice leather holster and you go forth in search of missing blue Volkswagen."

Tears welled up in my eyes. "Jeez, fellows, you didn't have to do anything like this. I don't know what to say."

21

"No need to say anything.  Our pleasure.  We ain't been sentimental in a long time, though, so you get out now 'fore we change our minds and twist your turkey head off."

## Chinese Firecrackers

I no sooner stepped out onto the street than I was wrestled to the ground by ten plainclothes officers and ten who were plainly overdressed. They took me to the office of the Chief.

The Chief said, "Frisk him!"

"What for, Chief? Everybody knows he never learned how to shoot a gun."

"Go ahead and do as I say. I have a hunch."

Of course they found my almost-brand-new .38 in its handsome leather holster.

"Aha!" said the Chief, "have this gun checked out by ballistics." And he tossed the gun towards his adjutant.

Unfortunately the adjutant, who had been a world-class racquetball player but had never played baseball, dropped the gun, which blew up, sending him through the wall into the coffee-break lounge.

"Chief," I said, "I wish you'd afford me the opportunity of expressing myself more often. I suspected foul play all along."

## The Only Surviving Hippie-Chick
## Of the 1980s

The Chief had me brutally beaten by the ten plain-clothesmen and the nine remaining overdressed officers. Then he had me tossed into the gutter.

Along came a girl wearing a beaded Indian headband. In every other respect she resembled Princess Caroline of Monaco.

"Please help me," I said.

"What could I possibly do?"

"Well, maybe we could go to your pad and smoke a little dope."

"Never touch the stuff," she said. "But perhaps you'd pick up a fifth of Seagram's Seven on the way. I've got mixers in the fridge."

# A Re-awakening

I mixed us a couple of triples and we sat around talking about Ted Kennedy.  I said I was afraid he would be bad for crime.

After our second drink, she said, "Why don't you take off your clothes and go lie on the bed?"

I complied, still feeling a little cheated in the Chinatown encounter.

She came toward me stark naked except for her beaded headband with a single feather.  When she got to the foot of the bed, she bent over and began sucking on my toes.

I shot my wad right through the goddam ceiling.

## The Nicest Thing Any Girl Ever Said To Me

"That's the only gun that counts," she said.

## Obligatory Beach Fuck

We walked down to Venice beach and got it on the twilit sand.

There was a lot of other fucking going on, but ours was probably the only case where rape was not involved.

It wasn't great either. She got sand up her pussy and I had a cold wind howling up my ass and almost lost my glasses.

Afterwards though we walked hand-in-hand by the purple surf and I said, "Isn't it a shame this can't last forever?"

"I hate to tell you this," she said, "but it's already over."

## What I Said Next

"How come?" I asked.

She explained that if she settled in with a guy she'd automatically forfeit her claim to sole remaining hippie-chickiedom.

## Back On the Trail Of
## This Missing Blue Volkswagen

"Well," I said, "I'd better hit the road."

"You don't have a car," she said.

"Christ Almighty," I said, "I used to have a car."

"What kind of car did you have?"

"If I remember correctly…it was a blue Volkswagen."

## What She Said Next

"I'd love to give you a lift," she said, "but my car was stolen recently."

"What kind of car did you have?"

"A blue Volkswagen."

## The New Paris

I gave the hippie-chick the name of the third best dick for her to hire to look for her blue Volkswagen. I was reserving the second best dick to look for my own.

I decided it would be fun to look for the original blue Volkswagen in Paris.

But since Long Beach is the New Paris, I took a taxi to my apartment in Long Beach and saved a few grand.

# A Realistic Touch

At home I realized I was in the throes of a godawful hangover.

Now, in the movies, dicks pull out of hangovers in half-an-hour with two aspirin and a cup of black coffee.

Bullshit.

I lay down, fell asleep for four hours, and came awake with a start. I was shaking and sweating and my mind was racing.

I took some valiums and threw them up.

I took a stomach pill and threw it up.

I wrapped myself in a sheet and sweat my pores dry.

It was afternoon before I could even face getting out of bed.

I went straight to the refrigerator for a beer and kept it down.

Then I took a shower.

I didn't feel like eating anything , but forced myself to swallow some toast.

I didn't know whether to chance some vitamin pills. Some people swear by them but, again, the problem is keeping them down.

If you're not having trouble keeping things down, you don't have a hangover.

Frankly it was a couple of days before I could even let myself think about Volkswagens of any hue.

## La Vida Es Sueno

On the day I finally felt capable of leaving my apartment, I decided to check out the state college campus. I stood in a parking lot couched in the lower doldrums. Strangely there were no VWs in the lot except for a blue VW van. The broad hadn't said her missing car wasn't a van, but something just told me so.

I always trust my instincts, most likely because I have very little else to trust.

Screams emerged from the van. They filled my ears like the earthen hues of a Gauguin tropical.

But I was almost sure the car I was looking for was not a van.

## La Vida Es Sueno Es Sueno

The parking lot was crossed by a serpent river. The parking lot was awash with Pontiacs, most of them on automatic pilot. Screams emerged from the back seats of the larger ones. In the midst of this a family was picnicking. The picnic made me hungry for potato salad, the kind my granny used to make, with lots of hardboiled eggs and celery and homemade mayonnaise. I used to wash it down with gallons of fresh lemonade, the tarty lemon cut by orange juice.

Perhaps it was the hardboiled eggs that made me a hardboiled dick.

No picnics in the era, though, the epoch of the missing blue Volkswagen.

## La Vida Es Sueno Es Sueno Es Sueno

I crossed the river to another parking lot. Here all the cars were Volkswagens and all the Volkswagens were blue.

But none of them was the blue of the original blue Volkswagen,that blue which I was sure was the elixir of intransigence.

## La Vida Es Sueno Es Sueno
## Es Sueno, Etc.

In the middle of the parking lot was a Bank of America. I entered it and stood in the longest line. I felt my hair growing whiter, my blood thinning rapidly. Soon my toenails would need trimming.

When it was my turn, I told the teller what I was looking for.

I was truly relieved when she didn't go into a Groucho Marx routine about telling the teller. One Groucho Marx per B-of-A branch is sufficient.

"I'll help you look for it," she said.

# Etc.

She slammed the window down on the
fingers of an old man with arthritis. Then she rushed
around front in time to stuff his mouth with deposit
slips when he opened it to scream. Around his neck
she hung an "Out to Lunch" sign.

We went outside. It was the sort of day you
associate with Dartmouth: lots of powdered snow
and candy icicles and a temperature of 75 degrees.

"My name is Little Nell," she said.

"My name is Bear."

"Be careful you don't get baited."

"I have been many times. Also I walk around
with perpetually bated breath."

"I'd like to buy some kleenex, Bear."

"Allow me to accompany you."

She led me to this gorgeous shopping mall. It
was called the City Centre Central Shopping Center.
There were fountains, promenades, boutiques,
sidewalk cafes—I felt I could live out my life in this
bucolic idyll, were it not that I had promises to keep.

We found the kleenex shop, which was one of
the largest in the entire complex, and she bought a
ten-cent box. Rather, I bought it for her.

# Etc., Etc.

"Let me buy you some lingerie," I said to her.

She led me to Undergarment Plaza where I watched her try things on. In spite of her name, she was a big girl, Junoesque, as they say, with one bad leg. Even her bad leg I found exciting. It wasn't that bad a leg anyway.

I bought her a sheer uplift bra embroidered with a single rosebud. I bought her panties so pastel they looked like they would melt in your mouth. I bought her old-fashioned things, like a black slip and a garter belt. I put it all on my credit card.

"Throw them old duds away, Little Nell," I said to her.

# Etc., Etc., Etc.

We walked around the parking lot. There were a lot of college guys going to and from their Porsches, and they all had eyes for Nell. I began to feel that she was more interested in strutting her stuff than in helping me look for the car.

"I think we'd better rest," I said.

"Where?"

"Right in here," I said, opening the back door of a shiny black Lincoln Continental with velvet upholstery.

"Aren't you getting in too?" she asked.

"I think I'd better drive us someplace more secluded."

We weren't more than a couple blocks down the highway before I heard her snoring gently. I drove us up to Portuguese Bend, to the cliff where the chickie run in **Rebel Without a Cause** was filmed. I gunned the big car towards the edge and performed my best last-second James Dean leap out the door just as she was coming to and mumbling, "Ummmm, a little snooze will sure give a girl a new lease on life."

I heard the vehicle explode on the rocks.

It was a long hitch back to the campus.

# The Campus Bulls

I went to the office of the campus police. It was known as the Department of Public Safety.

The officer behind the desk was big with a ruddy complexion with a bull neck. I told him I was looking for a missing blue Volkswagen.

He looked up at me. "That's good," he said. "That is just great. You know a lot of people who come in here aren't very helpful to us because they don't provide us with specific details. But you...you obviously have a pinpoint sense of observation."

"Thank you, Officer."

"How long ago did you take this case?"

"Oh, quite a while ago."

I noticed his cheek becoming slightly blotchy.

"A day, perhaps? A month? A year? Maybe in a previous incarnation?"

"I'm sorry but I don't own a watch."

"Come with me," he said.

# The Bulls, Etc.

I was taken to a bare room with a chair in the middle of the linoleum floor. Pointed at the chair were a cluster of ultra-bright lights. I was asked to sit in the chair. I was surrounded by peace officers. They were uniformly big, with ruddy complexions and bull necks.

"Look," I said, "I thought you guys all had college educations these days."

"We do," the ruddiest bull replied, "we were all fullbacks."

"What was the color of the car?"

"It was blue."

"Come on, don't give us that."

"It was blue."

Crack.

"It was yellow like the dried sperm of an aging Chinese laundry magnate, wasn't it?"

"No..." Crack. "It was..." Crack.

"It was green as the puke of an aging Irish fishwife."

"No..."

"It was red as the rhetoric of an aging Commie agitator."

"No..."

It was black and blue as the bones of an aging miscegenating..."

"No…"

"It was mauve as the velveteen leotards of Oscar Wilde."

"…"

"It was just peachy…it was a pink lady…it was Grand Chartreuse…"

"Okay," said the sergeant, "We will accept for the time being that the car was blue. Now just what hue of blue?"

"It was the blue elixir of intransigence."

"Are you sure it wasn't sky blue pink?"

"Yes."

"Wasn't it a little closer to the blue blood of a Bel-Air matron?"

"No."

"How about the blue grass of Kentucky…blue balls…varicocele…blue denim…blue moon…the blue bird of happiness…the man with the blue guitar…blues for Mister Charlie…Mr. Blue…"

"No no no no no no no no…"

Crack crack crack crack crack crack crack crack.

"It was the blue elixir of intransigence."

# Transition

"Take the motherfucker to the shrink."

## The Couch

How perfect! And here I had been living under the illusion that the immortal Sigmund was passé. I thought they had buried him along with the immortal Monty. How reassuring about things in general to be lying in a white bare room with moderate lighting upon a worn upholstered couch.

# Der Doctor

Der Doctor entered the room. He had no nose, eyes, or lips, but wore thick bi-focals. His ears were elephantine.

"Zo you are looking for a car," he said.

"Yes, sir."

"Yes, **Doctor**! I am **Der Doctor**!"

"Yes, Doctor."

"Oh hell, let's not stand on formalities. Just call me Ishmael."

"Is that your name?"

"No, but it's what they call me at der cetology conventions. By the way, what's **your** name?"

"Bear."

"Bear!!! Oh my God! Oh shit! What a terrible name! Haven't you ever heard about Bear, Man, and God?"

"Well actually…"

"You better call me Doctor."

"Okay, but…"

"Tell me about cars."

"What do you want to know?"

"I want to know what you associate with your cars."

"Where should I start?"

"You better start **ab ovo**. What do you remember of the cars in your life when you were in the womb?"

"In the womb? Nothing. I don't…"

"Well it's a damn good thing. Only der nuts and der nincompoops remember anything about cars from their days in the womb. Do you remember the car that took you to the hospital?"

"No."

"Jesus Christ, I may have to send you out for a side course in mnemonic devices. Okay, okay, what is the first car you remember?"

"I remember the car that took my mother to the hospital."

# Mother

"I was three years old. My mother was going to the hospital to have a goiter cut. I was going to stay with Katie, my aging housekeeper.

"I was all right until she went out the door. I was playing with the toy soldiers she had bought for me. My father was in the war. Perhaps I would be okay, but then Katie said, 'Come to the window; come wave goodbye to your mother.'

"Bad idea. I went to the window and my mother was going away in a taxicab. I began to cry uncontrollably, smashing my military toys. I was still under the illusion that I could alter reality with tears. I was convinced if I cried long enough and hard enough, either my mother would come back to me or I would be brought to her.

"I could not remember the point at which my tears subsided into sleep."

## Mother, Etc.

"How long has it been since you have seen your mother?"

"Quite a while."

"Longer or shorter than since the broad hired you to find her Volkswagen?"

"Longer."

"Do you miss your mother?"

"No."

"Then tell me more about der cars."

# A Dodge

"My father had a Dodge. It had running boards and was an incredible ugly shade of brown. It had a floor shift and he bought it from my grandfather.

"My grandfather was eighty years old and smoked White Owl cigars. On every holiday we brought him a box of White Owl cigars. He always acted surprised."

"Do you blame him for that? Do you consider your grandfather a hypocrite?"

"No, I don't consider him a hypocrite. What was he supposed to do, say, 'Oh fuck, another goddam box of White Owls. Don't you people have any imagination?' Anyway, he couldn't have said that because he didn't say 'fuck.'"

"Your grandfather didn't say **fuck**?"

"He didn't say **shit** either. Or **hell** or **damn**. He didn't say anything."

"Not anything?"

"He had a garden in the back yard and he said things about that. He had an old radio and he listened every Sunday afternoon to the ball games and he said things about the games but he never swore. I think my grandmother considered it a little sinful to listen to the ball games on Sunday and he may have also, but he allowed himself that pleasure.

50

I guess they probably considered the White Owls a little sinful also, but they must have decided that man is by nature a sinner and I think they cast themselves upon divine mercy."

"What is the most pleasant thing you associate with your grandfather?"

"Corn. He used to have corn on the cob whenever it was in season. His teeth were gone, so he would slice it from the cob in great long strips with a special silver knife and then he would butter it heavily and spice it heavily with pepper and salt. I would beg him to fix it that way for me also, but most of the time he wouldn't, because he would say my teeth needed exercise, but some of the time he would, and then it would be indescribably delicious."

"What else do you remember with pleasure?"

"I remember playing softball in the back yard with him and I remember playing Chinese checkers with him on the living room carpet. I remember I never beat him at Chinese checkers and he used to say that losing now would make me a winner later. But I have never won a game of Chinese checkers in my life, and I am also very bad at chess. I seem to lack the killer instinct...

"I remember eating grilled white hots in summer. You can only get them in my home town and in Germany.

"I remember hearing he was a lumberjack when he was young.

"I remember being warned never to mention in front of him that my father drank beer.

"I remember my grandmother, who had something terrible growing on her cheek…"

## Sundays At The Old Folks'

"But, on the whole, you recall the Sunday afternoons spent at your grandfather's with pleasure?"

"I recall them as being among the most boring hours of my life."

# A Pontiac

"I was sitting in my father's Pontiac. It was green and white. It was not a new car but I had been taught to say that it was 'new to us.'"

"Where was your father?"

"He was in the bar."

"Which bar?"

"Henner and Bennet's."

"Did your father always leave you in the car?"

"No, sometimes he took me in the bar with him. Whenever I ate there, I ordered either spaghetti-and-meatballs or veal cutlet with tomato sauce or some scallops."

"And which of these do you prefer today?"

"I am addicted to Italian food, although I am perpetually on a diet."

"Why had your father left you in the car?"

"I don't know."

"Did you mind being left in the car?"

"I hated it."

"Do you think your father was in there with a woman?"

"I hope so, but I doubt it. My home town was pretty uptight. You couldn't get away with shit there. I'm glad as shit I got out of there."

## The Only Time My Children Will Appear
## In This Book

"Do you have children?"

"I have five."

"Do you live with them?"

"No."

"Do you ever see them?"

"I see two of them."

"Did you ever leave them sitting outside of Henner and Bennet's tavern in your lost but formerly possessed blue Volkswagen?"

"I never leave them sitting in the car."

## Henner and Bennet's Revisited

A couple of miscellaneous detail concerning Henner and Bennet's bar and grill:

Whenever I had a stomach ache, my parents would order me a blackberry brandy. In those more innocent days, no one minded a father and mother ordering their kid a dram of blackberry brandy for a stomach ache. Blackberry brandy was universally touted as a remedy for stomach cramps and I, for one, would like to go on record as testifying that it always worked for me.

In fact, if anyone is listening, I would have no objection to appearing on television on behalf of the medicinal use of blackberry brandy.

But the TV racket is a tough nut to crack.

## The Advent of the McLuhan Era

Henner and Bennet's owned one of the first TVs in Rochester, New York.

Unfortunately, Rochester had no television station.

We used to try to get the station from Buffalo. Even though there was nothing much on except wrestling.

All we ever got was snow.

There we sat, the three of us, my parents with their bourbon-and-cokes and I with my blackberry brandy, huddled in front of Henner and Bennet's TV, the snow outside on our Pontiac, the snow inside on the TV screen.

## The Plymouth of My Aunt Matilda

"What car of your infancy do you remember with the most profound displeasure?"

"The Plymouth of my Aunt Matilda."

"Why?"

"Oh Christ oh Christ oh Jesus Jesus Christ…I could write a book about the Plymouth of my Aunt Matilda."

## Guilt

"Try to keep it to a thousand words or less."
"I may keep it to no words at all."
"What is the matter?"
"I feel guilt."

## The Advent of Guilt

"Do you feel guilt often?"
"For thirty years I felt no guilt, only fear."
"But now you feel guilt."
"Now I feel guilt often."

## A Devoted Life

"You see my Aunt Matilda made me her whole life. She has no life of her own. She would have given me everything, done anything for me. She still would."

"And yet…"

"And yet she drove and drives me up the wall."

# The Legendary Plymouth

"Let's stick to the legendary Plymouth of your Aunt Matilda."

"She drove me to the park. She drove me to the pool. She drove me to the golf course. She drove me to and from school.

"She drove terribly, slipping down in the seat like the last of the Bellflower low-riders. She was very seldom on the right side of the road. The only possible reason she is still alive is that she drove so slowly. There are few cars in Rochester that have not been sideswiped by the legendary Plymouth of my Aunt Matilda. More young men have died upon the streets of Rochester, trying to pass the Plymouth of Aunt Matilda, than have fallen in the rice paddies of Southeast Asia.

"She drove me everywhere.

"She drove me and still doth drive me up the walls."

## The Tail Of A Lamb

"When my friends and I were waiting for her to take us to the park, she would call from inside the house, "Be ready in two jerks of a lamb's tail.'

"We would stand outside the door jerking our little asses, but it never seemed to hurry her."

# Robert Valdocchio

"And it was always your aunt who took you to the park?"

"No, sometimes we were taken to the park by Robert Valdocchio's uncle, in his rakish tudor Ford."

"And this Robert Valdocchio?"

"He was the next door neighbor of my aunt's, and I spent a lot of time as a child at my aunt's house. He was four years older than I. He was not exceptionally strong or fast or talented in relation to the kids his own age, but he was always a little stronger and faster and better, and, of course, more confident at everything than myself.

"He seldom lost and he was not a gracious winner.

"We were 'friends' throughout grammar school, and I think we probably did have a great deal of love for one another, but the concomitant hatred was thinly guised.

"We were out playing in the dusk one Autumn, when he was just entering eighth grade, and he was chasing me in and out of the yard, and I knew that when he caught me, as he invariably would, I was going to absorb a middling beating. So I let him gain on me and then I fell in front of him and he tripped and soared through the air and landed

64

belly-down upon the stump of a sawed-off iron pipe. It put him in the hospital.

"I intended to trip him and I intended to send him soaring through the air, but I did not intend that he should land upon that pipe or on anything.

"I was scared shitless over what I'd done, but neither family seemed able to believe I was capable of such a deed.

"Afterwards, Robert claimed he might have been a great basketball star if it were not for missing the eighth grade team because of his injury. But he was never really any good at basketball. He usually beat me one-on-one by bullying, but I was better than him, although much younger.

"Robert Valdocchio, wherever you are, why couldn't you have let me win a game once in a while?"

# A Cheerleader Of Eros

"Please try to stay a little closer to the subject. Please return us to the legendary Plymouth of your Aunt Matilda."

"When I was in high school, you had to be eighteen to drive after dark. Consequently my Aunt Matilda drove me on most of my dates.

"I would be in the back seat with my date, trying to love her up a bit. I was bashful and inept and the girls were Catholic and ambivalent, so I wasn't really getting very far. But I was doing my best, everything considered.

"Matilda was always focusing on the rear-view mirror, trying to get a view of the proceedings.

"She never mentioned the goings-on in the back seat, but she sure did take an interest in them.

"At the time I was operating under the assumption that my Aunt Matilda was a maiden, but my family was notoriously close-mouthed, and I heard a rumor later, from someone outside the family, that my Aunt Matilda had been married at one time. So maybe she'd been laid once or twice. Or maybe he couldn't get it up on the wedding night and it was annulled. Those things were always happening in those days.

"At any rate, I never minded much her peering into the rear-view mirror, because I always felt somehow she was rooting for me."

## She Stuck By The Kid

"Later, after my first divorce, she was the only one on my mother's side of the family who didn't disown me."

## The Last You'll Hear Of My Aunt Matilda

"Look, I'm getting pretty sick of hearing about your Aunt Matilda."

"I can understand that."

"Is there anything more you feel absolutely obliged to tell us about your Aunt Matilda?  Or her legendary Plymouth?"

"Well…she just about drove my first wife up the wall.  She came to visit us in Tucson to help out with the second baby and she stayed three months.  She took the place over completely.  Both kids thought she was their mother.  She gossiped shamelessly with our neighbors in the apartment house.  She told them I had been a famous athlete back in Rochester, which was a good deal short of the truth.  One night I came home from a party on all fours pulling myself up onto the bed where I spent the night puking all over myself.  The next day she said to my wife, 'He never drank before he knew you.'

"Of course I had known the poor girl since puberty."

## A Platonic-Freudian Synthesis

"It seems to me that the quintessential blue Volkswagen may be parked somewhere within your childhood."

"Bullshit."

# Mounds

"Well, whatever's right. Let's hear a little more about the cars of your adolescence, attempting, as far as possible, to avoid references to your Aunt Matilda."

"I used to have my mother's Chevrolet for the asking, as long as I was home by dark. I used to park with the girl who became my first wife on the deserted back roads in the Scottsville-Chili area. Lots of poplars staunch against the sunset. Van Gogh would have liked it.

"Ironically, the most powerfully sexual moments were before we had begun to screw. Endless hours of sucking on her plump white tits. Endless hours of dilating her cervix with my middle finger. Tugging at her bra and tugging at her panties, yes no yes no, no no no, yes yes yes yes…

"Like Mounds bars, it was indescribably delicious."

## Earlier Bulls

"Once the cops pulled up and asked to see our licenses. My cock was sticking out of my pants and we were both under age, but they may have recognized my father's name because they didn't hassle us. My father was no big-wig, but he worked at the county penitentiary and knew a lot of sheriffs.

"Thinking back on the incident now, I'm surprised they didn't throw me out of the car and ball her themselves.

"The Fifties was an age of innocence."

# Sympathy

"Later, when we had progressed to more advanced stages, we would drive to my mother's house and fuck on my bed.

"But she always had to be seduced, because she had always been to confession and gotten herself cleansed of our most recent fornications.

"It was delicious seducing her, she was so young and partridge-like and hot and innocent. It would usually start with one of us rubbing the other's back...

"If my mother or Matilda arrived at the bottom of the hill, they would always honk their horn and we would scurry into our clothes.

"I don't know whether my mother knew we were fucking and didn't want to embarrass us, or whether she wasn't sure and didn't want to find out, or whether she thought I would get the fucking out of my system and decide not to marry the girl...or what...

"I suppose I should put the best construction on the situation and assume she was sympathetic to our sexual maturation.

"But she sure as hell wasn't sympathetic to our marriage."

## Un Autre Divorcee

"The only one who was sympathetic to my divorce and re-marriage way my Aunt Marilyn, the wife of my father's brother.

"My uncle had been married before and she was a Catholic, so she was happy to have another fallen-away-for-love Catholic in the family.

"She came to L.A. once and got in touch and I drove up to see her. She couldn't tell me often enough how badly she wanted to meet my new wife. I didn't tell her I was already separated from that wife also. It would have destroyed the whole Duke of Windsor flavor of her fantasies."

# A Cousin

"My Aunt Marilyn was also very concerned about her son, Duke. Duke, her younger son, had always been a problem. He was just about my age.

"He had been a terrible student all his life and had always been turning over her cars on the Merritt Parkway. Whenever he wrecked one jalopy she would buy him another and the next week there it would be—by the side of the road in flames. Everyone predicted a bad and early end for Duke.

"But then one day he turned over a car with a girl in it and she was partially crippled and he married her and cared for her and it straightened him out and he went back to school and got a master's in goatherding and a Ph.D. in history.

"It was the old O. Henry reversal of fortunes.

"But as soon as he had it made, Old Duke started to hit the bottle. He began beating his wife and getting picked up on drunk driving charges. He missed a lot of classes and his job was in jeopardy. He had started attending Alcoholics Anonymous, but then one night he showed up drunk and cracked a couple of skulls. Things were looking pretty gruesome for Old Duke, and my Aunt Marilyn, who was endowed with one of the finest pairs of tits in Long Island history, wanted me to tell her how to face up to this crisis.

"I tried to tell her that I am a drunk myself, but she wouldn't listen."

## An Arbitrary And Not Altogether
## Graceful Transition

I turned to Der Doctor and said, "Would you like to hear some more?"

I was answered by a vast and awesome snore. Der Doctor had fallen asleep in his chair.

I figured he must have been very overworked to have fallen asleep in the midst of such a scintillating narrative. He must not have had a wink for days. A shame too, because I had so much more left that I'm sure he would have found fascinating— like my trip across the country in an Opel station wagon and how that allowed me to visit every Buick repair department in Middle America. There were a number of vehicular romances I could have elaborated upon as well—from back in those days when I could still stretch out in something more compact than a Lincoln Continental.

Well, he'd just have to hear those tales another time.

## A New (To Me) Car

I snuck out of the Department of Public Safety and hitchhiked down the road to Huntington Beach. I figured I'd better pick up a new car and that the best place to get one cheap was from a surfer.

Sure enough the first kid I approached, board upon his head, was only too willing to talk turkey. We settled on five hundred bucks, I signed a check, and he handed me the keys to the car.

I drove it back to Paul's bar to see if I could dig up any more great leads like the Chinatown one.

# A First

"Gettin' any, Paul?" I said.

"Bear," he said, "last night was a first for me. This girl came in the bar and started bandying erotic terminology with me, and I thought she was just talking, but sure enough she stuck around till closing. So I took her home with me. Everything was copasetic until we got our clothes off and climbed into bed. Then I reached over and flicked off the light and she said, 'You can't stand to look at me, can you?'

"I guess it just rubbed me wrong because I said, 'Sure, you're not bad looking at all. It's your smell I can't stand.'

"And I threw her out of the house.

"I was glad in the morning that I had. It would have been an unholy odor to wake up to.

"But it's the first time in my life I ever kicked a piece of ass out of bed.

"In advance, at least."

# A Hot Tip

"Look, Paul," I said, "you got any leads for me?"

"What kind of case you working on?"

"I can't divulge that at this time. Just give me a lead."

"Okay—try the waterfront."

"The waterfront. The waterfront! Paul, that's a great lead! I'm off to the waterfront. Wanta come along?"

"I would, Bear, but I've got a sweet young thing joining me for an after-hours drink at Mel's. In fact, I've got to get these drunks out of here so I can lock up. Hey, you drunks, get out of here so I can close!"

Nobody paid the least attention.

So Paul said, "Bear, you'd better leave now," and he took a couple of canisters of tear gas from behind the bar, and then he escorted me to the door and flung the bombs back in.

In a couple of minutes he was able to lock up.

I waved to him as I turned my car towards the waterfront.

## A Waterfront Dive

I drove down Anaheim Street and turned left into the depths of Wilmington. I slowed in front of a bar that I suspected of being a genuine waterfront dive. Now that San Pedro's Beacon Street is gone, replaced by absolutely nothing, waterfront dives are hard to come by. On the sidewalk in front of this place stood a short, stocky man in a raincoat, lighting a cigarette. He was the spitting image of Mickey Spillane. As if to emphasize the point, he looked up and gobbed on my fender.

That convinced me I had indeed unearthed a true waterfront dive.

# A Question of Honor

In an essay called something like, "The Fine Art of Murder," Raymond Chandler once discussed his hero, Philip Marlowe.  He pointed out that one of the overriding principles of Marlowe's character was that he would suffer no man to visit insult or injury upon him with impunity.

Now I wish that were true of me as well.  I'd feel very good about myself if it were.  Of course I'd also be in federal prison.

And it **is** half true.  I always take revenge on anyone I'm pretty sure I can kick the shit out of.

On borderline cases, it's about 30-70 I'll let the matter slide.

When the odds are lopsided against me, I will only strike back when acutely intoxicated, when my children are involved, when a woman I am still insanely in love with is involved, or when it is an indisputable question of honor.

I considered Mickey's gobbing on my fender an indisputable point of honor.

So I parked the car, and on the way into the dive, I held one nostril shut with my finger, and snotted through the other on his shoe.

He was so astonished I was able to disappear into the murky bowels of the saloon.

## Within the "Yank 'Er Inn"

Murky? I guess it was murky. I no sooner plopped myself on a barstool than there were so many hands on my thighs I thought I'd stumbled into the octopus tank.

"What's your pleasure, sweetie?" the bartender inquired.

I slipped on a pair of brass knucks and answered, "My pleasure is beating up on queers."

Suddenly I had all the elbow room I could ask for.

I had one drink, strode magnificently to the door, checked rather tentatively to make sure Mickey wasn't waiting outside, and scooted to my car.

# You Know As Well As I Do
## What Happened Next

I drove a few blocks further and decided to try a place called the Isle of Lesbos.

I got about five steps inside before a fist came crashing into my chops.

I countered and decked my assailant.

"Look, lady," I said, "if you're going to be a man, you better work a little harder on the heavy bag."

She was crying.

"I'm sorry," I said, helping her up. "I didn't mean to blow your scene, honest. Look, my lip is bleeding."

"It is?"

"Sure, you pack quite a wallop. You get yourself down to the gym and you'll be knocking them dead in no time."

She seemed to feel a little better then.

"Now," I announced to the assembled patrons, "is a blue Volkswagen the sort of car that would be apt to appeal to a homosexual of any ilk?"

They didn't seem to think so.

"Okay," I said, "just one more question then. Are there a couple of you who wouldn't mind getting it on while I just sort of stood around and jacked off?"

The next thing I knew I was back in the gutter.

# A Peculiar Occupation

I drove out to the wharves, which were deserted except for an old man in baggy pants and tennis shoes who needed a shave. He was sitting in front of the immense dome of the Spruce Goose and he was writing something on a pad.

"What you doin', old fellow?" I asked.

"Just making my will."

"Oh, I would have guessed you'd have done that a long time ago."

"This isn't my first," he said. "In fact, it's my six hundred and thirteenth."

"I see. What kind of car do you drive?"

"To tell you the truth, I don't drive anymore at all. I kind of let my license expire. But I do have a private plane that I've meant for years to get some use out of. I'm gonna take it up as soon as I'm satisfied that I've drawn up the perfect will."

"Well, good luck, old-timer."

## What A Way To Go

I drove onto the Vincent Thomas Bridge, which I consider one of the world's most under-rated bridges, and I wondered why so few people commit suicide by jumping off of it.

I mean, people are forever jumping off the Golden Gate Bridge.

I mean, I've known people who drove all the way to Frisco just to jump off the Golden Gate Bridge, when we have a perfectly good bridge right here in Southern California.

I guessed it either just one more case of Angelenophobia, or else it was because the water is so filthy beneath the Vincent Thomas Bridge.

## The Ghost Of You-Know-Who

I pulled off the road at the Chickie-run. A middle-aged man with a fifties ducktail was walking back from the edge.

"Getting' closer every time?" I asked.

"Got it down to the shadow of a cunt-hair," he replied.

"Well," I said, "it's a hard thing to get out of your system. What kind of vehicle you leave down there tonight? Not a blue VW by any chance?"

"That's about the only model I **haven't** left down there," he said. "Tonight it was a '56 Bel Air. Not a bad car for the first twenty years."

"Give you a ride anywhere?"

"No thanks. I think I'll just mosey on down the hill to Point Fermin and sack out on the beach till morning."

"Not a bad life," I said.

"Not a bad death," he replied.

## Literature and Life

By now I was plumb out of leads so I picked up a paperback dick-story at a liquor store, drove up to the Pantry on Figueroa, and sat there for a couple of hours, reading the book and drinking coffee with lots of cream and lots of sugar.

When I put down the book, I knew the solution to the Case of the Missing Blue Volkswagen.

The broad had stolen her own car.

## Ah Shit I'm Not Done Writing And You're Not Done Reading

Now all that remained was to find the broad. Unfortunately I had no idea where to look for her.

## The Old Indentation On The Second Page Trick

So I stopped in the nearest bar and asked for a notepad.

I perused the top page closely and sure enough there was a message indented from what had been written on the previously torn-off page.

Someone had written, "See you at the Water-Polo Lounge."

## Cherchezing La Femme

So I drove down to the famous Water-Polo Lounge of the Barferly Hills Hotel.

The maître d' didn't care a whole lot for the looks of me, but I'd had the foresight to pull on my jacket and tie. As he was sending me to a table in the vicinity of the scullery, I stopped in my tracks and intoned, "Anybody here driving a Volkswagen?"

From the assembled producers and screenwriters and rubberneckers came a unanimous chorus reminiscent of the last movement of Beethoven's Ninth:

"Are you shitting me?"

## Little Big Man

I called over the dwarf who does the paging for the joint.

"You got a sister about six-foot-two?" I asked him.

He spun on his heel and departed.

## Lovers' Lane/Murderers' Row

I was so close to Mulholland Drive it seemed a shame not to drive out there and see if the broad had been murdered.

No, it wasn't likely that the broad had been murdered, but it was more than likely that her younger sister, if she had one, had been.

Besides, I'd never been on Mulholland Drive before.

I'd heard too many scary things about it.

# A Rocky Road

From Laurel Canyon to the San Diego freeway, the drive was fine, but after that it was horrendous.  The road was unpaved, full of ruts and rocks, a swirl of dust.

I had neglected to bring a six-pack, and I was reluctant to swill from my pint of Seagram's Seven for fear of dehydration.

My nerves were fucked.

It took me two hours to wend my way in sight of the suburban communities just off the Ventura freeway, and, wouldn't you know it, just as I had the drive about licked, I heard gunshots back up in the hills.

It took me another hour to reverse my trail to the scene of the crime.  The victim had been dead approximately one hour.  She had twenty-four bullet holes in the back of her head.

She bore a striking resemblance to the broad but was a couple of years younger.

I didn't want to fool around with the police just then, so I left my card on the body.  I figured they could call me at the office if they wanted to get in touch with me.

## A Question Of Taste

I passed Benedict Canyon but I didn't bother checking it out for murders.

Ever since Charley Manson, it's been considered to be in poor taste, even by homicidal maniacs, to murder anyone in Benedict Canyon.

It will probably continue off-limits for a few more years.

I suppose the homicidal maniacs, like every other profession, have their Ethics Committee.

## Spookeroo Town

You've probably noticed that in books the murderer is never a black person. That would be too easy a solution. Still there are many black persons in our prisons for the alleged commission of violent crimes and while it is incontrovertible that racism has often prevailed in our judicial determinations, it is perhaps not unreasonable to surmise that not all the black gentlepersons in our prisons are political detainees.

In other words, I decided I better pay a visit to Watts.

Now another myth of hardboiled fiction has it that all us dicks are real cozy with the shines, that we've got a list so long of informers and we have a great rep for fairness and no black individual or gang would ever fall upon one of us because of or rep for indomitable toughness.

Well, I didn't know anyone in Watts because I went there so seldom.

That's why I was the Best Dick, instead of the Best Posthumous Dick.

# The Blags Natch Café

I picked out the shabbiest looking joint in the environs of Main and Imperial and pulled up in front. On the way in I said to myself, "I bet I'm about to get my ass kicked."

I walked up to the bar and the bartender said, "Son, is there any particular reason on this otherwise pleasant evening that you've decided to get your ass kicked?"

"Look," I said, "just let me ask one quick question: has a tall white broad been in here tonight?"

"I ain't seen none," he said, "but if I had I think I can vouchsafe she wouldn't be so tall no more."

## The Palm Springs-L.A. Axis

Palm Springs would have offered a nice respite after Watts, but Palm Springs was a long ride on a windy road and I've never had the bread to eat there, let alone stay over.

God knows what kind of bucks you'd have to have to bribe any information out of anyone in Palm Springs.

Anyway, I decided if the solution to the case was only to be found in Palm Springs, then it would just have to go unsolved.

# California Living

Maybe the broad was a swinging single.

I drove to Marina del Rey and started pounding condominium doors. The development was known as Stonehenge.

At every door I pounded on, an off-duty stewardess answered.

Invariably I opened the conversation with, "I'm looking for a broad."

And I got many doors slammed in my face.

But not invariably.

I started alternating between three apartments of three stewardesses each, hopping hole-to-hole like the proverbial big-ears.

I stuck around a month before my exaggerated sense of duty demanded I return to the case.

## Obligatory Warehouse Scene

I got the Official Dick Manual out of my glove compartment.

After Swinging Singles, it said, "Try a warehouse."

So I drove to the City of Commerce.

The warehouse was about what you'd expect: falling crates that I sidestepped by inches, gunshots ripping holes in cardboard boxes, a runaway, riderless fork lift that barely missed unmanning me.

I stayed only as long as I felt was expected of me.

## Hard Guys Have Feelings Too

I was getting kind of nostalgic for the old days, when there was always a gambling ship anchored, beyond the coastal limits, off the shores of Santa Monica.

Now Santa Monica was only a place where you went to the hospital.

On a hunch, I hired a helicopter and landed on an offshore oil island. Sure enough, four guys from the graveyard shift were sitting around playing poker. I asked them if there'd been a broad around.

"Yeah," they said, "there was one who stopped by a couple of hours ago. Long, lean, sexy thing in a swimming suit. Said she was on her way to Catalina."

"Quick!" I said. "Abandon this island."

"Are you kidding? We're only on the fourth card."

I boarded the helicopter in a frenzy. "Take 'er up!" I cried.

When we were at about five thousand feet, the island blew sky-high.

I saw one of the workers go past the window. He was holding four clubs.

## You Oswald Spengler

In the Main Street gym I asked a guy with one ear if there had been any broads in.

"Broads?" he said. "Shit, all we got is broads."

I looked around. Sure enough, it was all broads working out. There wasn't a male boxer in the place.

"It's all anybody will come to see," said the man with one ear.

## Dick Hall

I went down to Dick Hall, which is not a used car dealership but a private club for functionaries of my persuasion.

They wouldn't let me in because I wasn't driving a convertible.

## A Find

Suddenly I had an inspiration.

I raced to Carpeteria and ordered the manager to unroll all their carpets.

Sure enough, about two hundred bodies came tumbling from those rugs, all of them clearly relatives of the broad.

But none of them was the broad herself.

# Obligatory Chase Scene

Fortunately I had a new box of business cards in the glove compartment, so I left one on each of the bodies and got out of there.

It was on Brooklyn Avenue that I realized I was being tailed by eighteen beaners in a woodie.

I hit the pedal and they chased me through Boyle Heights, Lincoln Heights, El Sereno, and Highland Park.

Along the way a few obligatory police cars swerved into a few obligatory baby carriages.

On Fremont Avenue in South Pasadena, they had the obligatory decency to carom off a bridge and land in the middle of the Pasadena Freeway.

## Obligatory Codger

It was time to consult the Official Dick Manual again.

On page 133 I read, "Codgers veritable data banks."

I knew the only place to find a codger was on a bench, so I repaired to MacArthur Park.

I pretty much had my pick of codgers there, so I took the Manual from my breast pocket: "Any codger will do. Seen one codger, seen 'em all."

Sure enough my codger, a cross between Walter Brennan and Barry Fitzgerald, said, "The broad? Of course I know where the broad is. She's being held captive in your apartment.

"**My** apartment?"

"Your own apartment."

## Mi Casa Es Su Casa

I decided it was high time I learned to use a gun, so I stopped off on the way home at my regular liquor store and said, "You got a gun behind the counter, don't you?"

"Sure."

"Let me borrow it for a few minutes, okay?"

"What if I get held up while you're gone?"

"I'll take the case for free."

## Mi Casa Es Su Casa, Etc.

I came into my apartment gun in hand.

Just as I anticipated, the place was messed up pretty bad.

Whoever had messed it up must have been some kind of an animal.

I saw a pair of eyes beading at me from behind the sofa.

I sunk four quick shots right between those eyes.

## The Culprit

I flicked on the light and approached the fallen interloper.

I had murdered a raccoon.

## La Vie Moderne

Screams issued from the closet:

"Let me out!  Let me out of here!"

"Admit that you're a trans-sexual!" I demanded.

"All right," she said, "just let me out of here."

"It's about time you came out of the closet," I said, unlocking it for her.

## To Err is Human

"You idiot," she said, "you've killed my pet raccoon."

"Whoops," I said, a bit sheepishly, "I thought it was a trained burglar."

"It was all I had left in life that I loved—what with my blue Volkswagen missing."

"Well, look," I said, "why don't you observe a respectable period of mourning while I return this gun. And try to have that stinking carcass out of my apartment by the time I return."

## A Crime Within A Crime

When I got back to the liquor store, the manager was dead and the safe was hanging open.

I went outside where two young men with stockings over their heads were trying to get their car started.

"Shit, man," they said, "a brand-new battery and it ain't worth shit. Could you give us a push?"

"I don't see why not," I said. "Could I give you a hand with that moneybag also?"

"Oh, I guess I can just swing it into the back seat."

"But if your car doesn't start, we'll just have to transfer it to some other car. Why don't we just set it over there by the wall while we see if we can get you started."

"Good idea, man. We'll hop in the car and you just give us a little push and if that doesn't work, then maybe you would lend us your car to go pick up our private mechanic."

"Makes sense to me."

They got into their car and gave me a little wave. I pumped my two remaining shells into their gas tank and the car went up like something out of Cape Canaveral.

I was beginning to get a kick out of this gun business.

## A Guy's Got To Make A Living

I extracted a thousand bucks from the moneybag as my reward and left my gun sitting on top of the bag with one of my business cards attached.

As I drove off in my car I heard sirens in the distance.

## Why Did She Have To Go And Name It That?

"Well," I said, "I'm glad to see you got it out of the house."

"You fascist," she said.

"What was its name?"

She said, "I called it **Nigger**."

# Crossing Out Items On A List

"Have you recovered my car?"

"Unh-unh."

"Have you tried every likely place?"

"I've tried all the places where Dicks ever find anything."

"Have you tried Disneyland, Marineland, or Knott's Berry Farm?"

"I'm sorry but I took a vow never to visit those places."

"The track?"

"I can't afford it.  I'm a lousy handicapper."

"The Queen Mary?"

"It's a nice place to look at but I wouldn't want to visit it."

"How about a nice lake—Arrowhead, Crystal, Big Bear?"

"Overdeveloped—not worth shit for crime anymore."

"Lake Isabella?"

"Perfect setting, but I don't feel like driving that far."

"Skid Row?"

"I might get mistaken for a bum by the police."

"A dog kennel?"

"A dog kennel?"

"I'm sorry. It just popped into my head. A stable?"

"A stable? What would your car be doing at a stable?"

"I'm sorry."

"You shouldn't be. Look, I'm just plain sick of driving around. Not even the Best Dick can get the whole goddamn city into one goddamn case."

## A Mysterious Phonecall

At this point there was a mysterious phonecall. The caller said, "Beware the woodwork."

"I think you must have the wrong number," I said, peremptorily hanging up the phone.

## The Eugenics Family

But sure enough, no sooner had I hung up the phone than they began coming out of the woodwork.

It was the sinister Eugenics Family, or, as they are sometimes known, the Seventeen Dwarfs.

# Their Names Were

Bimbo, Blottoed, Boobo, Bitcho, Bulko, Baddo, Bonko, Bippo, Bud, Blanko, Bloody, Blackperson, Blazingsaddle, Blackguard, Barfo, Belch, and Beaurigard.

## The Solution

Beaurigard, who was an amateur magician with a small following at the Magic Castle, whipped a Persian from a paper bag and flipped it out the window.

The broad sighed: "At least the cat is out of the bag."

## The Penultimate Chapter Before
## The Rediscovery Of The Missing Blue
## Volkswagen

"Where do we go from here?" I asked.

"We go," the broad said, "outside to your car."

## "You Imbecile," She Said

"How long have you been driving my missing blue Volkswagen?"

## Another Chase Scene?

I leapt into the VW and revved up the engine.

The Eugenics Family leapt into their seventeen stolen bumper-cars and revved up the engines.

I shut the engine off and got out of the car.

"Let's take a vote," I said. "Do we really want to go to the trouble of another Chase Scene?"

The vote went 19-0 (myself and the broad included) against a Chase Scene.

## A Corollary

"I can assume," I said, "that that includes no cornfields, cropdusters, parachutes, or speedboats?"

"Piss on the whole fucking rigmarole," said Bloody.

## A Settling Of Accounts

"Here," I said, "take the keys to your miserable Volkswagen. I was just getting kind of fond of it."

"What do I owe you?"

"Give me a check for $475.00. I need a car and I passed a '66 Pontiac Le Mans on the way over here."

"Money can never express my gratitude."

"Well, if you could get the Eugenics Family to turn their backs for a moment, I wouldn't say no to a little headjob over here behind this venerable oak."

## The End

"Another case brought to a satisfactory conclusion," mumbled Blottoed. "What do you do for relaxation between cases?"

"It always seems," I said, "that I have the woodwork to repair."

## About the Author

Gerald Locklin has published over one hundred volumes of poetry, fiction, and literary essays including *Charles Bukowski: A Sure Bet,* (Water Row Press) and *Go West, Young Toad,* (Water Row Press). Charles Bukowski called him "One of the great undiscovered talents of our time." *The Oxford Companion to Twentieth Century Literature in the English Language* calls him "a central figure in the vitality of Los Angeles writing." His works have been widely translated and he has given countless readings here and in England. He is a Professor Emeritus at California State University, Long Beach.